FAREWELL SPEECH

PROJECT BLACK BOOK VOL. 2
A NOVELLA

SHANNON EICHORN

What people are saying about the Project Black Book series:

"It's fun, it's engaging, and I got through it in one evening. I couldn't put it down. Definitely recommend!" — HodrosBooks.com, on *Farewell Speech*

"Body-sharing aliens, life-altering choices, and a mother's devotion—what's not to love?" — KM Herkes, author of *Rough Passages*, on *Farewell Speech*

"This book is so much fun...It's very kind to newbies, but with enough for veterans to fall in love with. Stargate vibes mixed with Stranger Things-esque teenage adventure with a dash of Tom Clancy and a healthy dose of pure love for sci-fi. Go buy it."
— HodrosBooks.com, on *Rights of Use*

Farewell Speech

Project Black Book Vol. 2

Shannon Eichorn

Astra Invicta LLC

ISBN 978-1-7324340-4-2

Cover Design by Dex Greenbright

Modified view of the Crab Nebula by NASA, ESA and Allison Loll/Jeff Hester (Arizona State University), acknowledgement: Davide De Martin (ESA/Hubble), included in cover art by Dex Greenbright

Trees and Milky Way photo by Noah Silliman on Unsplash included in cover art

Milky Way photo by Dns Dgn on Unsplash included in cover art

Contents

To Mom
with deepest gratitude
for all your support and bravery
in the years when it was just us

Chapter One

MATT

This was a bad sign.

On the kitchen whiteboard, Mom said she'd found a cure for aphasia and sent me to the couch in the upstairs family room.

I swallowed the lump in my throat and climbed the coarse wooden steps to the second floor. "That doesn't make sense. Your brain got miswired. You can't just take a pill for it."

I led her into the upstairs den, the converted bedroom that served as our family space for as long as I could remember. Mom used the big living room downstairs for her sewing business. She pointed to the tan couch that was older than me, and I sat.

She glared.

"Plunking down," she'd always called it. I was supposed to "sit like a gentleman." What a great start. (If a real gentleman had just come home after summer football camp and been summoned before he even had a chance to get a snack, he'd have collapsed into the seat, too.)

"Matt." She scowled. It was pretty much the only thing she could say aloud anymore, but she wielded her tone like a whole vocabulary.

"Sorry," I mumbled.

I rubbed my face. It sucked when Mom called me to the couch. It didn't happen often. Like when Dad died. When I started getting *D*'s and *F*'s in eighth grade. When she got back from the freak stroke and her own stay in the hospital the year after. Major things.

Mom perched on the far cushion, smoothed invisible wrinkles from her jean capris, and reached to turn on the lamp, even though the room wasn't even dark yet. She kept avoiding looking at me by studying a sticky note. Uh-oh. She'd prepared.

She reached for the upstairs lap whiteboard and started writing. <Met s.o. today, said she could cure aphasia.>

She'd met someone—s.o.—who could fix the damage the stroke left in her brain. Sure.

It would be cool. If she went through with this, maybe she could look me in the eye and talk again. Or we could call to each other from different floors. We could go back to trying to shout at each other in loud restaurants. Or we might drift apart when her phone calls didn't have to go through me.

I shook my head. "It can't be legit."

She wrote under her first sentence. <It comes with a job.>

This was the two in her one-two punch. She'd talked for years about getting a new job. Sewing wasn't a steady gig, but enough customers always came for us to get by. They must have, or we'd have had to move after Dad died.

<M, you know what this means?>

"No, go back. Who told you this? They can't cure aphasia. They can't just fix it. Everyone's been telling us the only thing to do is the therapy you're already doing."

She glanced down across the room at the flash cards under the TV. She hated them. She'd described—just once—how humiliating it felt to have to re-learn how to say words she'd been able to say aloud since she was a toddler. How to say words she could hear and write just fine. She erased the board. <It was one of Jo's associates.>

"From the Air Force?"

She nodded.

"Why would the Air Force try to cure aphasia? This doesn't make any sense. It would be so cool if you could talk again, especially that fast. You can get it back without them eventually. I know you can."

She ran her fingers through my hair then turned back to the board. <But if they can now? Isn't it worth a try?>

"It'd be amazing if they fixed it, but what do they get out of it? They're curing you *and* giving you a job? Sounds like indentured servitude." Like the kind of carp we talked about in history class.

<Ofcn.> Of course not, she meant. With a sigh, she wrote one more thing. <I'll see what they have to say. U can help me think it thru.>

<hr>

I didn't hear Mom get home from her big meeting with the... What did they used to be called before they were hacks? We heard about them in freshman history class last year. Snake oil salesmen. Charlatans. Quacks.

I noticed her in the dark family room as I was about to head downstairs for a mid-homework snack. She sat on the couch with her head in her hands in front of the lamp that made up for January's early dusk. Oh no.

"Mom?" I leaned over the couch back and hugged her shoulders.

She tilted her head against mine.

"What's wrong?"

She shook her head.

"How did it go?"

She waved her open hand—so-so—then gave a thumbs up. Good-ish. But she looked so miserable.

I circled the couch, sat down, and hugged her again. "Did you find out they were full of it?"

She dragged the whiteboard off the coffee table. <They can fix aphasia.>

"Are you sure they aren't just saying that?"

<They told me how. I understand.>

"So, it *is* indentured servitude!" Otherwise, she'd be thrilled.

<No, the job is very important.>

"Uh-huh." Sure it was.

She met my gaze and looked away. <I can't do it.>

"Why not?"

<It's asking too much.> She shuddered and shook her head. <It's a good job. But why me? Why seek out someone who needs to be fixed?>

You're fine the way you are. But I couldn't tell her that. Again. "It can't be that good of a job if they're willing to throw in that much medical expense."

<It's important.>

I couldn't picture her leaving her tailoring business. She loved it. But if it let her get back to normal... What could they possibly have asked to get her to consider turning that down? I couldn't ask; she'd said something about it was confidential. "What are you going to do?"

<I don't know. We need the $.> And she wanted to get back to normal. She tucked hair behind her ear. <It's a v important job. I wish I could explain.>

Whatever she wasn't telling me must have been a doozy.

<Savings are getting lean.>

"I can get a job!" I promised, jumping to my feet and rattling the DVD stacks and track trophies on the shelf over the TV. "I can get two!"

<Or I could get one.>

This was all so different when Dad was here. I swallowed against the lump in my throat. It was better when I didn't think about him.

She amended, <Doesn't have to be this one.>

"I could do it, Mom. I could help out."

<You keep up your grades and sports. You're looking for scholarships, Kid Com.>

Kid Commandos weren't old enough to need scholarships, but I'd stopped arguing about the embarrassing nickname after her stroke. Some things didn't really matter in the end.

She erased the board of her side of the conversation and sat straight. Then she stood up and pulled me into a hug.

We'd make it without the Air Force and whatever about their offer scared her. We always had before. Sure, maybe some things would have to change, but I was cool with that.

She sat and uncapped the marker again. <I'll tell the AF no.>

The doorbell rang on a Saturday morning in spring when I was reading in my room. I meant to ignore it and leave it to Mom until I saw a woman I didn't know getting out of Jo's SUV. Jo's coworker—it had to be.

We'd called them months ago. Mom said no.

I rushed halfway downstairs in time for Mom to open the door, its bell tinkling, and stand with a hand on her hip. I gripped the wooden banister so hard, its loose spindle supports tilted and squeaked.

I'd never seen Jo in fatigues before, her big attitude locked away under plain, drab green. Usually, she wore normal clothes—jeans, snarky T-shirt, boots, leather jacket. Usually, her smile took up half her face, but not now. Today, she stood stiffly, in uniform, expression grim. "I'm sorry to bother you, Mrs. King. Sarah needs to speak to you."

No more first names between Mom and Jo! I clutched the wooden banister tighter.

The new Sarah lady walked up behind Jo, her long, dark blonde hair barely peeking above Jo's shoulder. Then she stepped to the side, wiping her eyes and cheeks. She looked like a wreck, despite her neat business clothes. Her eyes were puffy and red, and stray locks escaped her haphazard ponytail, as if she was in high school and her senior prom date had just dumped her. "Can we talk one more time?"

Don't do it!

Mom held out a few seconds before giving in. She stepped aside to let them into the room that served as the public part of her sewing business, where Jo's boots squeaked on the linoleum that ran between the stairs and the fitting booths and between the front door and the kitchen. Mom cast me a plaintive glance as she reached for the down-stairs whiteboard.

As she closed the door, I rushed to the bottom landing to stand beside her and caught Jo's disappointed expression. They didn't want me here. Too bad.

<What's wrong?> Mom asked.

I cringed. That was the wrong question. It should have been *What are you doing here?* or *Didn't you hear me? I said no.*

Sniffing, Sarah edged in front of Jo. "I need you to reconsider." Her voice dropped to a whisper. "Please. No one else I've asked will even talk to me. You're the only one who might still..."

Preying on my mom. I crossed my arms, hoping I looked like a bouncer. "What's with the waterworks?"

Mom and Jo both glared at me. Sarah's lip quivered. She spared me a glance but focused on Mom. "Please. There's an opening. My best friend is dying. Please talk to her before she's gone. She can answer your questions. And if K—if her job's not right for you, it'll be— She'll be—"

She burst into silent tears.

"Excuse us." Jo steered Sarah into the corner to compose herself. She looked wrong crying by the waiting chairs and giant Easter Bunny on the wall beside the curtained changing booths. The big back mirror by the step riser showed Sarah's tears from another angle.

I leaned toward Mom. "Don't listen to them. They're just trying to manipulate you."

She wrote very small, which would be hard to read from across the room. <M, this chance isn't going to happen again for a long time. I can listen and still decide later.>

"You already decided!"

She winced. <I am still curious.>

"They're just trying to trick you."

She raised a skeptical eyebrow and nodded at the woman breaking down across the room. <They're not.>

"Can I go with you?"

She cupped my cheek apologetically. That was a no.

Jo and Sarah turned back, and Mom hurried to erase the whiteboard.

This time, Sarah held herself stiffly, hands clasped behind her back, expression controlled like she'd snapped out of her funk. Like she'd only been acting before, the manipulative quack. "Mrs. King, I can think of no better person for you to discuss this opportunity with than the woman whose position we're offering to you. This window won't last long."

Mom pressed her lips together. She watched Sarah for a moment, as if the newfound composure might crack. As if she couldn't decide if it'd been an act. Her knuckles turned white where she grasped the board.

The woman who'd come in crying hardly looked like the same person now. Her expression softened from stony to wooden. "Please. It will take us months to line up another candidate. My friend has days. Meet her and decide later. You two have compatible spirits."

Mom shook as she wrote her next question. <What about Matt?>

"It's just a day trip," Jo said.

Mom glanced at me, and I knew what she was going to say before she wrote it. <I'll go.>

Damn.

"Don't go."

Mom stopped screwing the lid onto her water bottle in the kitchen. I wasn't sure where Jo's base was, but Mom only took extra water on long drives, like out to Jo's rodeo. Mom's lips pressed together, and she finished tightening the cap. She ruffled my hair as she brushed past to grab spare snacks from the pantry.

"You already decided you didn't want to do whatever they're asking." I crossed my arms. "Is going with them worth it, even if they could help you talk?"

She crinkled the bag in her hands and stared into the distance. Then she shrugged slowly and, not even looking at me, passed me again to load up her tote.

"They're trying to manipulate you!"

She straightened up and blinked at me. Then she stepped close and wrapped me in a hug.

I stiffened. But it wasn't like when Dad was around. We only had each other now. I hugged her back. If she had a bad feeling about the Air Force's offer, she shouldn't give them another chance. She could stay here. Keep tailoring people's clothes. No one wanted her to be anyone but who she already was.

She let go and pulled the kitchen notepad across the counter. <I'll be back tonight. I ♡ u.>

I watched her get into the car, and it sort of felt like she was never coming back.

Even if I knew she would.

She'd said so.

Chapter Two

ILENE

Matt was afraid for me.

I thought about him during the whole long drive to Jo's base in the Montana boonies under the pale sky and through the budding green valleys between ruddy buttes. Like so many other times, it would have been a different conversation if I could have just told him not to worry, that I'd only go a couple counties east of Billings, that whatever I did, I'd make sure he was taken care of. If he could hear my promise in the tone of my voice.

I told him the important part.

I followed Jo's SUV across the green-dusted prairie and up the base's winding drive to the buildings that housed the core of what they called Project Black Book, the Air Force's program to defend the planet from threats from outer space. Then I followed Sarah into the big, stout building where she'd first told me about how she could bring back my speech by implanting an alien brain in my neck that attached to the natural brain in my skull. She'd assured me that the other brain came with an important job, something about working to defend Earth from behind the scenes. A steady paycheck sounded good, but sticking a living thing in my body? I'd said no.

Still, here I was, back to listening again in case something they said could tip the balance in their favor. In case I might agree to get my speech back after all.

Lila Wijesekara, my ombudswoman, met us at the door, cheery pink blouse brilliant against her dark skin. "Ilene, it's great to see you again!"

I waved, tensing as I followed Jo and Sarah.

"I'm really glad you're reconsidering," Lila continued, "but don't feel pressured. If you have any concerns about how this is going, don't hesitate to let me know. I'm here for you."

I nodded and pointed to Sarah, trying to convey that everything was fine, that I didn't need all this fuss.

We entered the dingy, white hallway that smelled faintly of grease and dust and industrial floor cleaner. Sarah's office was ahead on the right, where, as soon as they'd been allowed and I could take a day away from my business, she and Lila had flooded me with her offer's details and drawbacks. I'd spent sleepless nights the last few months wondering what I'd missed. Walking back toward it felt fated—fortunate or not, to be determined.

Before we reached Sarah's office, two soldiers emerged from a room on the left, guiding another young man between them in handcuffs. He looked out of place, wearing the same pants and boots as his escorts but a simple black T-shirt. The escorts' haircuts were buzzed short and neat, but the prisoner's hair was long and greasy, lying clumped together past his shoulders. He hadn't tucked his shirt. A thick, plastic collar, gray and overlapping in the front as if with a wide strip of Velcro, looked like a miniature version of a dentist's lead vest.

I stopped to watch as they passed. The prisoner waved his bound hands, and his escort nudged him to walk faster.

"Don't worry," Sarah murmured. "They're keeping a close eye on him. They know what to look for."

I blinked, frowned at her in confusion. The only odd thing—hardly threatening—was his plastic collar.

"Oh, sorry. He's Kem."

I waved her to expound.

She rubbed the back of her neck. If she hadn't shown me her scar when she'd explained it all to me, it would have looked sheepish. Instead, it reminded me of the creature living in her neck and stretched into her skull. "The Kem are kind of like our symbionts, the Gertewet. Except the Kemtewet completely take over and wipe out their hosts."

She'd mentioned the two kinds of aliens before, but I'd forgotten in the rush of revelations. I stiffened. It was one thing to hear about extraterrestrial life, another to get confirmation of alien predators.

She held her hands out as if to tamp down my panic. "It's okay. He's the only one on Earth. Years ago, Katorin accidentally brought him here from the Kem capital, and he took over one of the people guarding him."

Those guards that looked so burly and in control... If even they couldn't save themselves...

Sarah continued, oblivious to my discomfort. "General Marshall had to tell the host's family he died—and he did, effectively. His body's still moving around, obviously, but Cube Head—Katorin called him that because of his hairstyle in his last host, and he decided to rename himself—doesn't even remember his host's name. Everything that made Sergeant Rodriguez himself is just gone."

I suppressed a shiver at both her description and her alien's existence then pointed at her.

"Oh, Vinnet doesn't do that," Lila insisted. "All of us who work with Sarah and Vinnet can tell them apart."

The difference had been obvious back at the house. Sarah's body had all but solidified.

I pointed to myself and signed a K, since it was one of the easy ASL letters to remember.

"Katorin's like Vinnet," Lila promised. "She shares her host's body, which is why you'll be able to talk to Setira about what it's like to host her."

I glanced once more at the prisoner walking down the hall. A body snatcher—that's what the Gertewet and Air Force were fighting against. Really important work. My pent-up shudder escaped. The young man's collar clamped around the back of his neck to close the predator in. My skin prickled, delayed reaction to the threat that had passed. At least it was hours away from Matt.

Sarah stopped with her hand on a doorknob.

Lila brushed my elbow. "I understand this is going to be a personal conversation. But if you need anything, I'll be right down the hall."

I nodded, and she headed off.

When Sarah spoke, her voice was soft. "Setira is special. The Kem kidnapped other girls when they took me years ago, and I'm friends with some of them like Lila. Jo and her team have been amazing since then. But Setira was the only one I could celebrate being a host with. Everyone else who knew just tolerated it, even if they liked Vinnet."

I didn't know what to say—I was still working up to tolerance—but I put my hand on her shoulder, since I couldn't say anything, anyway. Clearly, Sarah loved this woman whose shoes she'd asked me to fill.

"Setira used to sneak me out of boarding school some weekends to do Earth things. We snuck into Disney World a couple times. It's a blast for polyglots! We started talking like we do at home on the base, but no one could understand more than half a sentence we said." Sarah laughed. "Vinnet fought it the whole time, even though my roommate said she'd cover for us. Setira wanted to see all the multicultural stuff. I wanted to do rides. Katorin was fascinated with the World of Tomorrow. 'Kem don't dream about the future like that,' she said. 'Not anymore. It's missing from their culture.'"

Hearing people's stories was my favorite thing about my sewing business. I lost myself in Sarah's memories until I remembered why she told me about her friend. I signed a K again.

"Katorin is going to need a new host. She needs to not be alone when Setira—" She choked up again.

When Setira died.

I was not agreeing to replace her.

Taking a deep breath, Sarah wiped her eyes and opened the door.

This room was the same size as Sarah's office, but a hospital bed took up half the room instead of a desk. A corner lamp glowed gently instead of the harsh fluorescent overhead. An old woman lay wrapped in the bleach-white sheets, her short, wavy hair wisping around an elongated head. An IV bag was tethered to her arm. She wheezed each time she breathed out.

Sarah pulled one old metal chair up to the bedside and waved me to it. Then she fished for the old woman's hand and held it in both of hers.

The woman stirred. Her head tilted toward Sarah, and her eyelids twitched.

We were too late. We had to be. I read it in the press of Sarah's lips, the tears that resumed their tracks down her round cheeks, the slack muscles in the old woman's neck.

The way her stillness recalled my late husband's last hours.

Sarah squeezed her hand again and lay it on top of the sheets. Then she reached for something on the counter in the back corner, a syringe. She held it in a vice grip like it might wriggle from her fingers.

She wiped her cheeks, but it didn't slow the tears.

I touched her arm and frowned at her. The old woman didn't need any help dying. She'd almost finished on her own.

Sarah took a deep, shaky breath. "This will buy you a few hours to talk. But then that's going to be it."

I pressed a little on her arm, as if it might keep her from advancing on the old woman. With my other hand, I dug for a pen and notepad to ask what she meant.

But she got the hint. "She'll die."

She's already dying. And if lying semi-conscious in bed for the rest of time was the alternative, it wasn't much quality of life. <Did she choose this drug?>

Sarah closed her eyes, and her lip quivered. "She chose to come here to try to talk to you. I just— She was always so old, she seemed immortal. I don't want her to go."

I knew that feeling. My husband was supposed to grow old with me. Together forever, we said. The only team we needed.

I rested a hand on Sarah's shoulder and stood with her as she sobbed.

The woman on the bed moved her head, lolling toward us. Her eyes fluttered, barely opened, and she reached weakly for Sarah's hands. She rolled one crooked finger in a circle as if to say keep going or hurry it up.

Sarah sniffed, took a deep breath, wiped her face, and stood very still. Composing herself, maybe, or suddenly coming to terms with mortality. Everyone did, sooner or later, one way or another.

I rubbed her shoulder gently.

She wiped her face again and finally glanced at me, but her expression had shifted, drained. What remained—the alien's expression, I guessed—wasn't as hardened as it had been at my house, only muted. Her eyes pinched in stress, but the tears had stopped. She shifted her grip on the syringe and inserted it into the IV line. When she spoke, her voice was smoother. "Setira will feel energized for no more than a few hours. She will rapidly decline after that."

It was strange listening to another personality using Sarah's mouth. So much life drained out of her when the alien took over, it seemed obscene. Exactly what I didn't want to happen to me. What I didn't want Matt to have to watch.

Sarah's alien, Vinnet, pulled something from a bag under the chair and set it on a tray over the old woman's lap. Silver and flying-saucer shaped, it was only about a foot across and had a deep hole in the middle. She—it? the alien?—tapped its silvery surface, and a light projected from the top. She held a finger in front of the camera, and a holographic fingertip the size of her torso hovered over the device. Space magnifying lens. Fancy. "Setira will need help reading your handwriting. If she needs more than this, you may call me back in to interpret, or I'll send for an overhead."

An overhead? I pictured days in my youth when teachers hand wrote with markers on plastic and projected in front of classrooms. Surely, the alien meant something else. I nodded.

She leaned over the bed, brushed the woman's cheek fondly, and fluffed her pillows. She pressed the back of her hand against the woman's broad forehead and tightened the sheets around her shoulders and neck. Fussing. The stony, reserved alien cared, too, in her own, subdued way.

She cast around the room for more busywork and seized on a knitted, purple blanket folded at the foot of the bed, unrolled it past the tray table, and smoothed it over the pale form. She murmured as she fussed with how it lay, "Katorin, when she wakes up, tell Setira we brought Ilene King to meet her. She's uncommitted at this time. She has aphasia, and I thought you might be able to supplement her language processing. Her son sounds like the kind of family you prefer to stay involved with."

The woman nodded once, still wheezing as she breathed. She glanced at me and then relaxed back again with her eyes closed.

Vinnet finished with the blanket and cast around for something else. She adjusted the position of the silvery space magnifying lens, glanced at my notepad, set out a spare pad and pen, and seemed to run out of available tasks. She sat down. "No one understands what it is like to live with a symbiont better than their host, with respect to both benefits and drawbacks."

<Besides speaking and having my body taken over?>

Her lips tightened. "Sarah says I'm inflexible but a good companion. Setira will tell you definitively, but I've heard Katorin's prior hosts describe her as fun. They laugh a lot."

Fun for real or by comparison? I doubted I could deal with sharing anything with Vinnet. <What do you know about Katorin?>

Vinnet smiled. It was small, subdued like everything else about her, but immediate. "Katorin is a good friend, kind and generous. All her hosts loved her, though usually as friends before they reached this point. She's been a lifelong friend to me. Setira's family passed before she joined us, but Katorin still visits her prior hosts' families. She is a legend among them."

<And her drawbacks?>

"Katorin can be impulsive," Vinnet answered.

"Good impulsive," a voice croaked from the bed. The woman held her head straight, her eyes open, studying me.

I sat a little straighter.

Vinnet launched back to standing at the old woman's side. "Are you well?"

She gave a tiny shrug. "Katorin says I'm as well as can be expected. I feel better than I have in weeks."

"It's only going to last—"

"I know." Setira, Katorin's host and the old woman I could see, caught Vinnet's hand and squeezed it. "Let me talk to Ilene while I can. Sarah, it'll be okay. Listen to Vinnet."

Vinnet leaned down for a brief hug and then stepped past me. "We'll be outside if you need anything."

The door shut behind her, and my tether to normality snapped. It'd been nice to have someone familiar in the room.

I tried to focus. My pen tip hovered over the lined paper, frozen. I didn't want what she had to offer, but I had come. I wanted my speech back. I wanted to know what I'd miss by continuing to say no. I hoped for a job without having to compromise myself.

"You haven't been around us much," Setira observed. "You're skittish. Katorin won me over slowly. We partnered for years until her previous host died. By then, I liked them both, and I couldn't lose Katorin, too."

<I'm not doing that.> I held my notepad up to the magnifier, and it projected a holograph of the paper almost as large as the bed.

The alien woman shrank the hologram size. "It's too late for you to build that founding friendship. Every single host has a different story. Vinnet's previous host hunted her down to volunteer. Teresh's host requested the first available symbiont. Hartwin's came through a matchmaking program."

I didn't know any of those people, but there was one other host I knew. <Sarah?>

Setira winced. "The Kemtewet kidnapped her. Vinnet saved her. I suppose if you were going to host, it'd be because Katorin made you feel less alone."

Alone.

I hesitated. It didn't make sense that I felt so alone these days. I'd had the house to myself many days while my husband was alive, even times when he and Matt had left on trips together. For now, Matt still lived with me. I wasn't alone, per se.

But I felt alone. The weight of having to make it all work fell on my shoulders. I couldn't tell Matt every scenario that could wipe us out financially. He was only a kid. I made the best choices I could, but we had only my income, only my car available for groceries and school, only me to run all the errands and make all the calls that kept life moving. Every fear I'd confided to my husband now lived pent-up in my head, where they got the zoomies in the wee morning hours.

Could a symbiont help with those raging thoughts?

<How can you be less alone if you're still only in one body?>

"I've found it doesn't matter how many bodies are around. Sometimes, the mind decides that it's alone. For me, Katorin is the only one who could ever break through that barrier, and she's never compromised my trust with that privilege." Setira shifted the magnifying projector as if she might turn it off, but she settled it back into place. She fidgeted, too. "You should talk to Katorin. I want her to go to someone kind."

<Of course.> But there were plenty of kind people in the world besides me.

Setira nodded, leaned back, and closed her eyes. It was an odd time to fall asleep, but she was old and clearly stressed. Maybe the medicine wasn't lasting as long as expected.

I sat back in the clunky, metal-rimmed visitor's chair that might have predated the missile silos dotting the countryside, the Air Force's less secret Montana presence.

It would be nice to not be alone, and I had other options if that was all I wanted. I could date again. If I could find someone willing to put up with me having to write every comment. Or if I could relearn all the speaking skills the stroke had robbed me of. If I could trust the impossible: that another man existed who I could love as much as my husband.

There'd never be another like him.

"Ilene?" The voice was the same, but the accent changed. The old woman suddenly sounded much more American, if still clearly born abroad. Katorin.

I stood, waving and hoping I looked friendly.

"Sarah means well, but she hasn't thought this through. If you only wanted to speak again, you wouldn't be here."

I crossed my arms.

"You'd head to your med clinic and get it fixed. A little memory loss would be worth it."

My hand shook as I wrote. My script appeared jagged in the hologram. <Your clinics can fix aphasia? What memory loss?>

"When was the last time you had a physical backup? Your physician should do one during every visit."

A backup like a computer? <How would that even work?>

"Your intake teleport should get saved to your file—at least your neural state. Everything else can be reconstructed."

<My doctors can't teleport. Are you saying yours could fix me?>

"Oh, right. You're from Earth. Of course you don't have a backup." Katorin closed her eyes and sighed. "I'm sorry. I forget how different

Earth is. Still, coming to the Gertewet for a physical ailment is overkill. It's like moving into someone's house to borrow a cup of water."

I wouldn't consider it if I had options. Well, if it felt like the flash cards might help me build back my spoken vocabulary. If I didn't have a dozen other fires to worry about, all worsened by not being able to talk freely *right now*. <Can your doctors fix me?>

"In extreme circumstances, they could have teleported in a backup copy of your brain or a section of your brain, but you don't have backups. I think Vinnet's wrong about you being able to speak because I can, but hosts do usually learn languages from their symbionts, so I expect your ability to speak will improve rapidly."

This was it. A ticket to being heard again. I swallowed against the lump in my throat. <How rapidly?>

"Maybe a couple years."

So fast.

"Standard years," Katorin amended, "so in Earth time, maybe under a year."

Hell yes.

"But that is moving into a house for a cup of water."

<Been living in a desert.>

"That doesn't mean you can ignore all the other implications of the new household."

Like the roommate. I shuddered. <Aren't I the homeowner?>

"Different analogy, but yes. It's like inviting someone to move in with you to wash dishes. Hopefully, you want them there for other reasons, too, or as Sarah says, it's going to get awkward." Katorin tucked her hands together and swam her thumbs out to the sides, an unmistakable awkward turtle.

"Matt!" I scraped my wits together to reply coherently instead of letting every cogent word get changed into my son's name between my thoughts and my mouth. <Where did you—?> Sarah. I scratched out my false start. <Why did—?> But I didn't know how to end it.

It shouldn't have surprised me so much that an alien picked up teen culture. I'd learned plenty from Matt.

Katorin's shriveled lips stretched around pristine white teeth. Then her smile faded. "Did I do it wrong?"

<No! I didn't expect you to know something so specific from Earth.> If she might move in to wash dishes, I had better find something to like about her as a person. Besides her openness to teen culture. And her ability to help with aphasia. <You must have spent a lot of time around Sarah.>

"Vinnet has been one of my closest friends for ages. When Sarah returned to Earth after her first mission, Earth had her under close observation, and the Coordinating Council sent me to keep in contact with her. She needed a lot of emotional support. The circumstances under which they met were not ideal for either her or Vinnet."

That didn't fully mesh with Sarah's relentless rosy picture of the Gertewet. <That happened when Sarah was a teen?>

Katorin nodded. "She was barely an adult by Kem society standards, a child by Earth standards, and a victim of the system to us."

I held up a hand. <What do the Kem have to do with—?>

Katorin explained before I finished writing, "Most humans in the galaxy grow up under Kem rule, even most Ger hosts. Ger don't have children except those our hosts have when they join us. So, most of the galaxy would have seen Sarah as barely an adult, even though Earth considered her a child for years after she began hosting Vinnet."

Sarah must have been around Matt's age when he lost his father, shortly before the stroke. Both Katorin and I had supported a teen after massive life changes. <You helped her recover.>

"Every new host leaves someone behind. Sometimes, their loved ones are lost to being Kemtewet hosts. Sometimes, even without Kem control, their loved ones turn on them. At best, the new host chooses to leave, and we can still keep in contact with their original communities. For Sarah, hosting Vinnet isolated her from her family. Even more so, Earth's inane order to keep knowledge of life *in the rest of the galaxy* secret isolated her, even when she was with her family. Vinnet's company helped, of course, but they both needed a friend to understand."

<To vent to?>

"To empathize," Katorin agreed.

<My son Matt is depending on me for that support.> Not least because I leaned on him for support, too. I swallowed. <With his father gone and how much I need his help now, it's been too much.>

"If you joined us, Vinnet could support him."

I shook my head as I wrote, <He needs stability.>

Which he wasn't going to get, not with my savings dwindling so steadily and the way I was soon going to have to decide between groceries and the mortgage payments. Thank heavens the football parents had pulled together to sponsor his equipment.

"Vinnet is assigned to Earth. She has the whole Black Book community supporting her."

Including Jo and the other officers who'd brought their uniforms for me to fit over the years. But I didn't know them that well. Jo was a friend but not close enough to ask for help. Matt didn't know any of them except in passing. My fallback plan had been to move in with my sister in Colorado, who was at least family, even if Matt barely knew them.

<Matt only has me.>

Katorin's brows furrowed, but she smiled. "You must be important to him."

<I'm his mom.>

"I'm glad you have each other." Katorin balled her fit and relaxed back into the pillows, her eyelids drooping. "I look after my hosts' families, but I understand if you aren't ready."

Of course I wasn't ready, but the mortgage didn't care. Even if we had to uproot and move states, though, finding a job there meant I could still be present to support him.

<If I took this job, it would cover our bills. It would change everything.>

Katorin winced. "Bills that you pay with money?"

I nodded, heart suddenly pounding in anticipation of bad news.

"We don't have American money, aside from what the Air Force pays Sarah."

I swallowed. <They could pay me, too.>

"We only need one liaison to Earth." Then Katorin shrugged. "But I can ask Sarah to pay your bills, and I'm sure I have some things rattling around at home we could sell on Earth."

Pawn off alien trinkets? I bit my lip. It could definitely work if anyone knew the real source, though I couldn't imagine the Air Force being pleased. Maybe to someone who already worked for the Air Force. Maybe to Jo or her base. Still... <What's the point of a job that doesn't pay?>

"The work needs to be done. Someone has to stop the Kemtewet from enslaving every human in the galaxy."

I thought of the mismatched young man in the hall and shuddered. <If you do that for free, how do you pay your bills?>

"For starters, we wouldn't charge our own people for food and shelter. It would be counterproductive. That's a Kem custom, a way to subjugate their own populace. They don't even charge their humans for that." She shook her head. "But we've all had undercover jobs as Kem and sent money home for operating funds. If Vinnet has been budgeting like that, she likely has savings that can cover for you. Or one of the other hosts from Earth."

<But that's theirs.> And I'd proven savings weren't a long-term solution.

"We can find a viable path forward together. We don't have to do it alone."

I touched my pen to the paper, but no words came. This wasn't a problem for later, like Katorin suggested. Getting my speech back would solve one issue, yes, but it wasn't worth selling my body for. The prospective paycheck might have been. The illusory paycheck. For the unpaid work. I blinked. <You said there's only one liaison to Earth.>

She nodded. "Vinnet."

<Then what would I do?>

"I'm often a courier to Vinnet and others in the field. I don't think we'll pull any longer assignments until we're acclimated to each other."

Assignments. I shivered. <What kind of assignments?>

"We call this a war, but it's not like the wars your planet has. Truthfully, we don't have the people or equipment to go head-to-head with the Kemtewet, so we place operatives in key undercover positions. When Sarah joined us, I was working as a convenience food designer on the Kemtewet capital world, collecting public information and looking for a missing operative—I found him, by the way! Since then, I've run messages from the base to Vinnet and operatives on the Kemtewet colony worlds. It's usually pretty easy for me to get in, make some new friends, make contact, and get out. I've had some elicitation gigs lately, too, where they send me to get info out of strategic targets. That's really my specialty."

A spy. They'd glossed over this detail in focusing on their need to overcome the body-possessing Kemtewet. My knuckles grew white around the pen. My mother had talked about what things were like when she was making her way, the fears and conformity in the 1950s. People ousted as spies died. My stomach churned.

"I'm very good at it." Katorin smiled, seeming to mean to be reassuring.

Good for her. <But it's dangerous.>

She lifted a bony hand and waved that off. "My last host, much like some earlier ones, died while I was making a go at Third Lord. There won't be much need for that anymore. It's a long-term investment, and we don't have all that much time left. We have plenty of other operatives who specialize in that—way more than the, let's see, in base ten, twenty-five lords' positions."

<Not much time left?>

"By our standards. You'll probably be my last host, but that doesn't mean our time together will be short."

So, she must have been almost as old as she looked. <It still sounds dangerous.>

"It can be, but all of us who are still alive are very good at what we do. We've had our close calls, of course, but we've learned from them. We lose people very rarely now."

I tapped my toe, waiting for the rest of the truth to drop like when Matt only gave me half a story. Katorin made it sound no riskier than Jo's job. Maybe only a little worse. Of course, she was downplaying it. <May I ask how old you are?>

Katorin blew out a breath. "Let's see... Six thousand and change, but your years are short, so more like two thousand, plus or minus your weird base ten math."

Oh. This alien had been alive during Ancient Rome. She belonged in a museum, not a mother.

Katorin winced. "I know. We're old."

<How long at war?>

"Oh, about twice as long before that." She shook her head. "I am probably not as old as you think. Those adjustments make a big difference for large numbers."

I waved her off this time. That was close enough. Maybe she was justified in feeling like she could navigate her undercover missions safely. She'd clearly done it for longer than I could imagine. But that left an even more important matter. I swallowed. <What about Matt?>

This would be the real final nail in the coffin of my speak-again-quick scheme.

"I can request a family hiatus. Hartwin has granted it before many times. I think he expects it of me anymore."

<How long?> Long enough for Matt to finish high school, maybe college? How old would he have to be for me to leave him on his own? *Never.*

"Certainly a few years. I doubt I could negotiate more than a decade." She smiled but still wheezed faintly when she breathed.

Years to see Matt safely settled. What a relief! <He still needs my support.>

"You'll do it, then?"

My throat tightened. <I,> I wrote. I wasn't ready. This still felt half-baked. Speech and a chance at paying my bills in exchange for my entire body. It still didn't add up. <I'll think about it.>

She nodded, wheezing harder. "Take your time. I just need...a minute to rest."

The corners of her eyes pinched tightly, as if she warded off tears. She lolled against the bed like she'd barely held herself steady all this time.

I pushed back to the wall, where the indestructible chair rim hit against the abused drywall, and hoped four feet was enough distance to think. My gut still said no. Katorin's reassurances hadn't soothed my churning stomach.

Katorin had supported Sarah after she got an alien implanted. Sarah lived with massive secrets—secrets I would have to keep, too, after all the nondisclosure agreements I'd signed. The way Matt sulked when I left this morning, this offer had clearly already come between us. If I went through with it, we might have only the shell of a relationship afterwards.

I'd see him safe, but I'd lose my son. I'd still be there, though. He might come around eventually.

Even if Katorin's borrowed finances fell through and we had to move in with my sister, I could still get my speech back, lift the burden off Matt to speak for me, find another job, and be there to support him.

He still needed me.

Not that he was the only one. I glanced at the bed again, where Katorin had fallen asleep, her curly white hair frizzed around her long head. She breathed with a soft, worrying wet rasp. She moved and chatted with a vitality that utterly vanished in sleep, leaving only her protruding bones and wrinkled skin that sagged around what must have been healthy muscle and fat not long ago.

Katorin needed somebody, too. But there were millions of somebodies out there. Even after he graduated, Matt had only one mom.

He didn't need his mom involved in a spy war, even as a courier.

Katorin coughed, and I jumped.

The old woman rolled to her side for a hacking fit. As it subsided, she held still, her deep breaths still wet. She looked up and waved me closer, speaking again with her thick accent, "This is Setira. I'm sorry I can't read your words right now, but listen. Katorin won't tell you this, so I'm going to. I'm going to die, and she'll be alone. There's no one here who will consider taking her but you. She'll be alone in her grief and isolated in a kaxan or the lifeport—"

Her rapt attention slackened, and she rolled away from me. "I'm sorry." The accent was diminished. Katorin. "I still need more rest."

I shivered. The symbiont had cut off what her host was saying. That didn't seem like her, except that Setira had said what Katorin clearly wouldn't.

Katorin didn't want me to think about her emotional needs, because she wanted mine to come first. Only Setira was thinking of her, and Katorin was planning to brave the grief of her death alone.

Like I had.

I leaned my head against the wall and stared above the foot of her bed at a bland picture of three planes passing a cloud, labeled *Leadership.* I knew what it was like to go through that grief while trying not to put it on the people who needed your support. It was hell.

I flipped to a new page in my notepad and wrote a question. Katorin feigned sleep when I slipped back into the hall.

Sarah sat in her office in the adjacent room, her door open wide, head piled on her arms on her desk. The glaring overhead light was off, a single desk lamp glowing but directed against the wall. It almost hid the tear tracks that glistened when she looked up and brushed her cheeks dry. "Mrs. King."

She reached for another blocky, metal chair, inching it closer by way of invitation.

I angled my notepad under her nose. <Are you going to support Katorin after Setira dies?>

Sarah's lips trembled. "I'll try. But she'll probably go back to the base. I need to be here."

<She'll be isolated?>

Sarah looked away. "If you don't host her, she'll have to wait in the lifeport until we find someone else. She'll be able to talk to anyone on the base, though."

<What does she do in the lifeport?>

"If she's not actively talking to someone, she can read through files. Vinnet says Katorin writes letters to her family and convinces others to deliver them. Vinnet has a memoir started. It's kind of a thesis on why someone should host her, but she's probably never going back to it."

<And?>

Sarah shrugged. "That's it. It really is boring."

Isolating, Setira said.

I hadn't seen Setira and Katorin interact, but they shared a head, a body. If Sarah was relaying Vinnet's comments, Setira and Katorin probably talked like Sarah and her alien seemed to. And Setira had been pleading on Katorin's behalf, because she knew Katorin would be alone.

I knew how that felt. Too many mornings, I had woken up by myself in a too-big bed, surrounded by too many closets and clothes my husband would never reach for again. I'd lasted three weeks before I'd had to pack away his things and fill the closets and drawers with other clutter. The emptiness where he used to be was unbearable until new stuff and routines filled in the gaps.

Katorin wouldn't have that. Only the part where she woke up to silence and her own miserable company.

<Is there somewhere I can be alone?>

Chapter Three

ILENE

Sarah claimed the conference room for me and closed out herself and everyone else. Odd to have the big room to myself with the massive, polished wood table and ranks of padded, black swivel chairs. Nice furniture, but the walls had been hastily repainted, leaving mismatched specks on the ceiling and wayward prints on carpet worn half-bare in the pattern of traffic around a different arrangement.

I hunkered down in a seat at a corner of the table, where I could see anyone come in before they saw me.

Odd to think that any of a dozen of my past sewing customers could come through, that any of them might look at home here, where I felt so out of place.

I flipped my notepad to a blank page. It would be cruel to leave Katorin locked away from even the meager connections of her uncaring world. Not that she was my responsibility.

Matt was.

The fact that I couldn't speak had shifted such a heavy burden onto him.

The fact that we never planned for my sewing business to carry all the household expenses... That we'd relied on my husband's job, and he wasn't around to win bread anymore... That we hadn't planned for him to die young... We'd had a healthy savings before, but I'd stretched it as far as it would go. We wouldn't be able to pay the mortgage much longer.

We couldn't stay in our house.

I laid an arm out on the smooth, cool table, and rested my head.

Whether or not I went with Katorin, my life would get upended. Katorin said she could keep Matt's life stable for the years it would take him to get started on his own—and connect him to a steady network beyond then. It was more stability than I could provide on my own.

A fresh start sounded kind of nice.

I cradled my forehead in one hand, elbow on the table, and stared down at the page.

Katorin seemed to have everything I needed.

It came with downsides, of course. Besides having to share my body—if I could come around to that—it brought a new person into the house with Matt. Sarah had *said* Katorin kept in touch with family, had painted her as a caring and supportive person. I even got that impression from how she talked about Sarah. But one never really knew. By the time Matt met her, it would be too late to back out.

I couldn't protect him from something controlling my own body.

<It's too risky for Matt.>

That decided it.

I tugged my sweater closed and ventured into the hall to show Sarah.

The empty hall was silent except for the soft buzz of the fluorescent lights. Sarah's office door stood open. When I knocked and showed her my notebook, she pulled out of a thousand-yard stare and frowned at the page. "Hosting Katorin will help you keep Matt safe."

Would it, now? How convenient to dump this bullshit when she shirked her own responsibility to support her supposed best friend after her loss. I crossed my arms.

"Really. We told you the Kemtewet take humans as hosts without permission. What we didn't tell you is that we strongly suspect the Kem are preparing to invade Earth. If you're with us, Katorin will know how to get Matt somewhere safe. Without her, you'll be on your own with no offworld access."

I gritted my teeth. Awfully convenient timing here. <What will you do?>

"Vinnet and I will do whatever we can to help the Air Force stop the Kem. We won't have time to look out for my family, but no one would fault you if you did."

Sarah cowered back, maybe from my expression. "I'm not just saying that. I've thought it through: Who would I want to sneak off Earth when the Kem come?" She glanced to the side. "I'd want my parents and my mom's dog and my high school best friends, Maggie and Lauren, and Jo and Fairfeld, and pretty soon, I might as well just stay and defend the planet, because you can only really fit six people in a kaxan. But I'm not a mom. Maybe you'd be happy to take just Matt. Katorin would help. She's taken a lot of her hosts' families to safety."

Sarah barely looked old enough to be out of high school; she clearly didn't have the wisdom to hear how she sounded, grasping at straws as she came up with solutions for Matt's safety. All I could see was a manipulative kid who waited until I declined again to tell me this key information.

<I need to talk to Katorin.>

Katorin was well and truly asleep when Sarah let me back in. The holographic magnifier had canted off her lap, so I set it on the table and out of the way for her comfort.

She stirred, and I patted her shoulder to encourage her to rest.

"You're back." She pushed herself up straighter and, coughing, reached for the magnifier I'd just put away.

Sighing, I returned it and tapped it on the way Sarah had. Or Vinnet. Close enough.

Katorin or Setira—whoever it was—nodded her thanks and cleared her throat one more time. "I'm sorry my host tried to guilt you into accepting me. My troubles are not yours unless you accept them. I'll get through. I have before."

<Your friends should help you.>

"They do, as they can. Their assigned work is important, too." Katorin drank from a glass at her bedside. "I hope that isn't what brought you back."

<Sarah said Matt would be safer if I hosted you.>

She balled her gnarled hand into a fist. "She shouldn't have done that, either."

<Said the Kem are coming to Earth.>

"That's not a datum for grounding a relationship."

Sarah hadn't meant it to be. It felt like she wanted somewhere for her friend to live without taking responsibility for supporting said friend. <Is it true?>

"That's not a healthy thing to base your decision on."

<Is Matt in danger?>

Katorin's bony shoulder pushed up. "We don't know. Sarah probably told you about the Kem plan to annex Earth, but it's unclear what they intend afterward. They could decide to leave it largely untouched as another farming world for raising humans. Or they might have enough symbionts ready to immediately implant most of the population. We haven't infiltrated enough to determine."

My heart pounded in my ears. <What if they did want to implant? What would happen to my son?>

Katorin leaned back and closed her eyes. "If he didn't escape, he'd probably be bought by some young Kem and implanted. He'd feel a burst of pain, lose control of his body, and then be trapped inside. To those of us watching, he'd basically be erased."

That was not happening to *my* son. <How likely?>

Katorin slit her eyes open to read my response. "It's foolish if they truly want to make more hosts available. If they're racing to make sure Earth can't destabilize the Kem Empire, they might simply wipe it out that way. It depends whether they see Earth as the credible threat we believe it is."

<If you were in their shoes?>

"If I had that power, I would free all the planets in the Empire."

<If you were the Kem?>

"In their mindset and objectives, the minimum success would require wiping out Earth's major military and educational institutions. The Kem haven't reset a population on that scale in millennia, and they'd have to do it much more quickly than before. Otherwise, Earth contrariness and resourcefulness will draw them into the kind of long-term struggle like ours but orders of magnitude larger. After great losses, they'll learn they need to immediately subdue a large portion of the planet. Earth will become a very upsetting place to be."

<How are we protecting my son?>

"I don't think this is the right reason..."

I tapped the question.

"Whenever you want, we can move him to a safe planet that's been a refuge to my hosts' families for generations. They screen their traffic. No one lands who isn't permitted."

<No Kem?>

"Never."

Heavens alive. A tension in my gut eased. After the months she'd had to tell me about this, it had been rude of Sarah to reveal the danger to Matt when she did, but Katorin not only agreed with me but also confirmed the danger was real. And she had a plan to keep Matt safe. <Matt can only go if you move in to wash dishes?>

"I'd like to decline to answer."

I perked up. <Can you move him without me?>

Her sigh degenerated into a short coughing fit. "If you return to your normal life, the anti-Ger forces in Earth's bureaucracy will impede our progress and accuse me of abducting you or your son. If you move him, that's simply a parent's prerogative. A loved one's. Any one of us would defend your decision to Earth's authorities."

So, it wasn't completely arbitrary leverage. Katorin didn't even want to tell me. She was actively trying not to pressure me. I had the measure of her now.

This was someone I could work with. For Matt. For myself.

I grabbed her hand, squeezed her cold fingers, and smiled.

Her eyes grew wide and round. She understood, even without words. "Are you sure?"

I nodded my head. Matt's safety could seal the deal almost as surely as Katorin's resistance to using it to pressure me, but I needed one more conversation first. <Almost. Need to talk to Matt.>

Her amber eyes shone with tears I hoped were joyful. She laid a hand on my upper arm. "Thank you! I understand. Thank you for reconsidering!"

I gripped her back and kept smiling, even as the dread settled into me like the cold from her fingers. There'd be no going back if I went through with this.

Chapter Four

ILENE

Katorin asked to see Sarah alone, so I waited in the shabby, bright hallway between pictures of a strangely angular jet and the biggest satellite dishes I'd ever seen in a vast, open field. It felt a little like a letdown to be set aside so quickly after such a big and scary decision. I was tentatively okay with letting Katorin into my body; didn't that make us besties? But, logically, I understood. The time left was too short for the depth of Sarah's and Setira's relationship, which would never be satisfied with what it had.

I leaned against the scuffed drywall, told myself I wasn't responsible for cleaning the long streaks marking the floor, and let my mind wander.

In the grand scheme of things, it was all too sudden. I'd known Katorin for less than a day—even if I thought I had the measure of her—and I was going to let her "move in to wash dishes"?

What a nice euphemism. I was going to let her live under my skin. Connect to my brain. Like a leech or a heartworm, some other creature feeding off my body. Best not to think about that too much if I really was going to go through with it.

A person, not a parasite. That's all I had to remember.

Sarah's sobs carried through the closed door. I pretended not to hear. Even with an alien in her head, Sarah was only human, barely an adult. She couldn't handle this kind of loss impassively, nor should she have to. Even Katorin certainly didn't make Setira impervious to emotional pains. I still couldn't tell how much either human host had changed because of their symbionts.

But I could find out. Wandering down the hall, I found Jo Patrick's office and knocked.

"Ilene!" Jo's broad smile flashed before the expression faded into a professional mask I'd only seen before when her coworkers crossed paths with her in my shop. She leaned against the doorjamb of a clean office, where a single one of her several rodeo ribbons shared an eggshell metal shelf with thick, official-looking binders. She blocked the rest of the view. "Is it time?"

I shrugged and nodded, not really sure. <Did Vinnet change Sarah?>

Jo pursed her lips to think. "The company we keep always rubs off on us in some way. They've spent a lot of time together."

<In bad ways?>

Distaste flashed across Jo's face and smoothed into a smile. "Sarah's become more pedantic over the years, but she grew up, too. I don't know. I was around her for five minutes before she started hosting Vinnet, and that was a long time ago."

<Setira?>

"Didn't know her before." Jo crossed her arms. "Are you worried about something?"

<For me?>

"Ilene, you're good people, and they're good people, and you can help with each other's problems. I can't answer whether it's right for you or what will happen. What you do is up to you."

<What would you do?>

"I'm not playing that game. It's your life. The Gertewet do good work with us. You do good work with your business. The decision is yours." She tapped my arm, and the grin returned. "You'll make a right call."

As if any path were good instead of all paths being bad.

She nodded down the hall, and her grin faded. "Let's see how they're doing."

I followed, her earlier words still ringing in my mind. *A right call.* As if there wasn't one perfect standard I needed to live up to. As if I could decide on the basis of which option brought more joy. Like not having to carry the weight of my life alone. Like being able to talk again. Like knowing that even in the face of this monstrous threat, I'd be able to protect my child.

I needed to see Matt again before I committed to it, even if we couldn't discuss it openly the way I wanted.

Jo knocked softly before easing into the room of Setira's death watch, and I followed close behind.

Setira/Katorin lay back, eyes closed but breath rasping. Sarah sat with her, clasping her hands. She glanced at us, face again streaked with tears, but continued murmuring whatever reflection she was telling her friend. The cadence sounded like a story.

Jo crossed to Sarah and settled comforting hands on her shoulders. I found a second chair. We waited together.

It didn't take long, maybe an hour at most. Everything fell silent. Then Sarah keened softly, and there was a faint squelching sound. Sarah jumped up, scooped something from behind Setira's neck, and rushed by. I barely glimpsed what looked like a purple, legless sala-mander.

Then it was just Jo and me and Setira's body with a splatter of blood seeping into the pillow around her neck.

Jo pulled the sheet up over her head and turned to me, mouth set in a grim line. "Thanks for staying."

I nodded. Then, thinking of that squirming creature in Sarah's hands, pointed to the door.

"Oh." Jo chewed on her lip. "I'm sure Katorin won't mind if you hold her later, since she let us hold one of the other symbionts once. I'm not sure she's in the mood for it at the moment."

I swallowed. *Hold* that thing? I'd only wanted to confirm what it was. That blood-streaked salamander looked more likely to slither down a sink than to wash dishes. And it got implanted in one body after another.

Jo rubbed my arm. "Hey, I know they're freaky. I have a hard time remembering that's Katorin, too, but it's the same person you talked to earlier."

Strange to think of that little creature as a person. It had been easier when she was shaped like a person—a human. When she'd stoutly decried anyone coercing me. When her knobby hands formed that awkward turtle.

I scribbled a question. <If, after I talk to Matt, I do want to proceed, what's next?>

"You can't tell him anything."

<Ofc not.> I sighed, glanced at Jo's confused expression and rewrote: <Of course not.>

"Think it over. We'll be here. Sarah said they sent everything they need with Katorin. If anything changes with them, I'll call you."

I squeezed her hand thanks and started toward the parking lot and the long drive home.

I left the base late enough to navigate by the stars, if only I knew which was the direction I wanted to go. (Besides taking the highway west. Road signs in headlights worked for that.)

The stars looked different now, and not just because I could see them between the glare of the base and the muted shine of Billings. They used to look so cold and distant, untouchable and unknowable above the shadowy buttes and rolling foothills. Now, they pressed too close. Katorin and Vinnet came from one of them. If I joined, someday they'd send me from star to star. And from one of those stars—or maybe many—a threat could encroach on Earth, on Matt's life. They said I could help stop it.

Who could stop the stars?

I shook my head and squeezed the gas pedal, watched the speedometer climb to eighty-five, ninety.

Surely, the stars went on burning, as indifferent to alien lives and wars as they were to us looking up at our Big Sky. No one had to stop the literal stars. It took people to stop Earth's World Wars, and it'd take people to stop an alien one, too.

But it didn't have to be me.

Or it didn't have to be now, no matter what Sarah said. I only had to decide faster than the next person offered this opportunity, and after that, Katorin would buy me time with my son in which I could talk with him—aloud, in full sentences—again.

My foot eased up on the gas, steadying out at ten over the not-quite-fictional speed limit.

The stars and predators glared down as I drove.

When I closed out the chill spring air with the front door, Matt perked up from the throw pillow he'd wiped the first-floor linoleum with. If he'd just had a little more patience, he could have ambushed me in the upstairs family space as easily. I still needed to go to bed, too. He snatched the pillow up like I might not notice and squinted blearily. "What time is it?"

I tapped my wrist for my usual signal of *late* and reached for the whiteboard. <Y still up?>

"Waiting for you."

I loved his sweet moments. I gave him a thumbs up, pointed at him, then mimed being asleep on a pillow.

"You're not doing it, are you?" He'd mastered pleading brown eyes, but they usually didn't work on me anymore. Not too often.

I hesitated over the board. *Of course not* wasn't fully true. Nor *maybe*. Every response felt wrong.

"Mom, there's more to it. There's gotta be. They're just going to cure you and give you a job? Why you and not everyone else you've passed at the doctors' offices?"

Because they wouldn't all get along with Katorin.

I froze. What an odd thought.

It seemed obvious now that Katorin and I would have values in common, but Sarah had looked desperate enough that anyone would do.

"You're the only one who might," Sarah had said.

Everyone had turned her down, so she asked me again. I thought I was her last resort, that no one else she'd offered to would even answer her calls.

"You two have compatible spirits," Vinnet had said. It sounded like bullshit. Empty words.

Had she actually considered that I might befriend Katorin so quickly?

Surely, anyone would have. Maybe not *everyone* in the waiting rooms, but certainly a few. Those few didn't all happen to know Jo Patrick, who introduced me to Sarah.

It really was just me.

"Mom?"

I tapped the marker on the board then wrote slowly, testing out the thought. <I think they knew I might be a good match.>

"And?"

<Still problems to work out but confirmed I can stay here with you.>

"Good..." He drew the word out, wary of my narrowly avoided fears. "They finally told you the fine print."

I nodded.

The fine print: the Kem were coming for Earth and my son someday, and while hosting Katorin would empower me to protect him, Katorin refused to manipulate me with those facts. She'd have us address each other as people, not positions to be plied with leverage.

And they didn't pay squat. My leverage on Katorin, I supposed.

Matt hugged the pillow to his chest, and his voice wavered. "Do you want to do it?"

<I have a lot to think about. Let's talk in the morning.>

I woke before the sun from a dream in which I caught up to Matt from behind and turned his shoulder, only to find his face replaced with the Kemtewet man's I'd seen in the hallway yesterday. Dream interpretation couldn't get any easier than that. My subconscious latched onto the threat of body-snatchers arriving on Earth to target my son, despite not knowing who I was or how far away we were from anything that might catch their initial interest.

Except the Air Force base defending against them.

Even if I didn't help Katorin, an invasion that targeted the base first would stumble on us early. We lived only a couple counties away—close by Montana standards, let alone for someone coming from another planet.

I threw off the covers, and the shock of cool air flushed away most of the dream's last grasping wisps. I tied my threadbare robe over pajamas and padded down to the kitchen for coffee and breakfast, extra conscious of each step of my morning routine. If I joined up, Katorin would surely change some of my comfortable habits. She could be allergic to coffee. Or perhaps slept in the nude. I'd had tense spats learning to live with my late husband, but with the opposing mind in my body, I wouldn't be able to slink away, get my sulk out, and cool off. I wouldn't have the joy of being surprised by a tender expression afterwards or a warm, engulfing hug. No kissing to make up.

No make up sex. So much for recapturing that in my next intimate relationship.

I poured my bitter coffee and carried it to the wall of family photos I'd studiously ignored the last few years in favor of the birdfeeder out the window. My parents and in-laws smiled...our wedding photos, Matt's baby pictures and early steps. First day of school. Happy days, moments in otherwise unremarkable days when the camera preserved broad smiles. Photos clustered in eras, and even if this era—when Matt and I forged on alone—hadn't been memorialized, it was coming to a close.

I needed something from this time. I pulled the digital camera from the back of the junk drawer and set it on the kitchen whiteboard as a reminder. We'd had a million worries keeping us from capturing new memories, but there were good things, too. I'd cherished this time with Matt, even if our losses had overshadowed it.

With the last sips of coffee, my gaze settled on a more recent photo of Matt, proudly decked out in his sponsored football uniform.

I could keep him safe.

I could speak again—in under a year! With no more flash cards and no more shame.

I'd have to join a war to do it. Eventually. Once Matt was settled.

But in the meantime, Katorin said she could convince Sarah—Vinnet, actually—to save our house.

And I'd have a companion. A true partner again instead of leaning on my child. That, a woman might thirst for with her soul.

With a second cup of coffee, I pulled a kitchen chair to the memorial wall and drank in the silence and fond memories while my thoughts swirled around the drain of a single decision.

A heavy thud upstairs announced Matt's return to the waking world. I swallowed. I'd expected at least another two hours to collect my thoughts. More thuds ensued, eventually scrambling down the stairs, until Matt stood in the kitchen doorway in his father's old hoodie that needed the cuffs hemmed, the one my husband had gotten on our first vacation as a family. The only thing of his father's Matt still touched, as if everything else hurt him too much. Matt stared like he'd expected me to have left.

I waved and sipped.

"What are you doing with the photos?" He shook out of his trance and scooped up the whiteboard, frowning at the camera as he set it aside.

I leaned to set the mug on the corner of the kitchen table. <Think we need a new one.>

Ended that with a definitive period. No questions.

"Why?" His voice barely wavered.

<Been a while.>

He settled on the other side of the table and looked at the wall with me. "I guess. Are you going to go through with it? You didn't answer me last night."

<Was thinking. Still am.> I pulled my chair back to the table, facing him, and set the coffee mug safely far away from the clunky whiteboard. <Know the fine print now + the benefits.>

"What benefits?"

Companionship came to mind first, but I couldn't tell Matt that, nor that it would keep him safe. <Pay the bills. Try something new. Talk.>

"And the fine print?"

If I told him nothing, he'd call it indentured servitude again. I didn't have the heart to tell him it didn't even pay that much. <Long commute. Long-term commitment. Relatively low pay.>

As long as Katorin bargained with Sarah to make sure Matt ate and had a roof over his head, we really could make this work. Katorin had sounded so sure. How much livelier would this morning's solitude have been with her?

"So, it's indentured servitude."

I raised a censuring eyebrow. <It's a solution to a lot of problems.>

"Like what?"

I bit my lip as I scrawled, <Money. Speech. Stable home situation.> My solitude.

"We can find another way."

<This is what I want.>

Oh.

I'd written the words hastily to win the discussion, but they echoed in my heart. It wasn't supposed to be about what I wanted. It was supposed to be about what he needed. But I'd minded that already, hadn't I? My wants aside, this was what could keep him safe.

"Oh." Matt fiddled with my mug, twisting it in stuttering circles before he would at some point sneak sips from it. "Well, if you'll be happy."

Tears blurred my vision. <I'll be here. We will. Together. Talking again.>

He sniffed, possibly managing his own tears. "Alright then."

I blinked and pulled him into a hug. He held me back like he meant it for once. *We'll be okay. And I'll be able to tell you that.*

After a minute, he slipped away and pilfered my coffee. "Now what?"

I had one more question, and I had to make it sound unrelated. <How would you feel if I dated again?>

He laughed and shook his head. "Whatever. That's your business, Mom." Then he wandered off and, miracle of miracles, poured his own mug of coffee and refilled mine.

I texted my sister to arrange her help during the surgery and emailed Sarah to answer some last-minute logistics questions, such as whether I should drive afterwards. (She said it would be fine.)

We took the photo of just the two of us and our tentative smiles.

All too soon, everything was ready.

Chapter Five

MATT

I brushed past Aunt Emily and sprinted upstairs to my room, where I watched Mom's car all the way to the end of the street. It paused at the stop sign then disappeared behind bare tree branches and houses as it crossed Yellowstone Avenue.

She wasn't leaving forever.

She'd said she'd be back tonight.

Outpatient brain surgery. Who knew?

I leaned my forehead against the cool glass and closed my eyes. The draft off the window brushed the back of my neck, and I shivered. This whole thing still didn't feel right.

On the one hand, Mom had sounded more hopeful than she had in a long time. Whatever this was, she wanted to do it.

On the other, the photo with her felt like she was making sure I had a last memory with her in case anything happened. And the situation still didn't make sense. The Air Force had no reason to be experts in curing aphasia. There weren't quick fixes to aphasia. According to every doctor we'd ever talked to, this offer she was accepting was bunk.

But she said she understood how it worked.

Fine. If someone was going to scam her, I needed to document evidence.

I pulled a half-empty English notebook from last year off the shelf of Hardy Boys and Dirk Pitt novels with old school supplies jammed on top. I flipped to the back and titled the page, <Evidence of Quackery.>

Chapter Six

ILENE

"Would you like to hold Katorin?"

I shifted uncomfortably where I sat on the sterile bed in the room where Setira died and pictured trying to cradle Setira's stiff body in my arms. But Sarah had brought only a thermos-sized container this morning, small like what she'd carried out in her folded hands when her friend died.

Sarah hugged the steel container closer. "It can never mean as much before, of course."

Pressing my lips together, I swiped my notepad from the nearby countertop. <Did you hold yours before?>

She stiffened and shook her head. Her mussed hair and deep under-eye bags made her the picture of regret. "I, uh, couldn't reach Vinnet. But I saw her. Those memories are important to me now."

Knowing I might regret it, I held out my cupped hands.

Carefully, she flipped a switch on the canteen, cracked it open, and lifted out the purple salamander creature I'd glimpsed smeared with blood at the back of Setira's neck. Sarah caressed its length with her thumb then gently tilted it into my palms. A tepid creature, heavy for its size, it had a head like a snake and skin like a frog. It curled into a muscly, violet ball and met my gaze. With what looked like immense effort, it winked at me.

I scrunched a signed *K* with one hand and raised an eyebrow at Sarah. *This* was Katorin? It was barely longer than my fingers, not even as wide as two fingers together.

"That's her. She." Sarah's weak smile faltered, and she grumbled, "Whatever, Vinnet."

That whole smiling, protective personality, not even filling my palm. Cool and slimy. She winked again and rolled in the smelly fluid that had dripped off her.

"She's drying out." Sarah offered the container to it—to Katorin—who rubbed affectionately against the base of my thumb before plopping back in.

My stomach knotted. But this was going to be the way through.

Sarah capped the cannister and flipped the switch. Then she paused, clutching it close. "I'm really glad you're hosting her."

I nodded.

Sarah stood in silence and wet her lips as if trying to say more. Sometimes it was nice when others struggled to speak, too. Finally, she muttered, still looking away, "I've found something sacred in the relationships between symbionts and hosts, and I hope you will, too, especially with your symbiont. I hope..." She squeezed the container tighter. "If you ever need someone to talk to about it, I hope you know I want to help."

Sacred. Not the word I expected from her. Or for this situation. Nothing about it felt sacred to me, but I nodded anyway.

Her smile didn't reach her eyes when she turned to the counter, set the container aside, and laid out tools from a kit. When she spoke again, she sounded more confident, back on track. "When you're ready, I'll put you under before making a small starter cut on your neck."

I raised an eyebrow.

She amended, "Actually, Vinnet will. She's had a lot of practice."

Such reassurance. She still looked like a teenager. But if Katorin was ancient, Vinnet probably was, too.

Someone knocked on the door, and Sarah frowned, opening it.

Lila burst in—wearing brilliant green today—breezing past Sarah to land a too-friendly pat on my shoulder. "Ilene! How are you? I heard you decided to host Katorin."

I forced a smile and a nod.

"Sarah forgot we have one more form for you first."

Behind her: "I didn't. I checked."

Lila ignored her and presented me with a clipboard and a warm paper that still smelled of toner. A list of statements with checkboxes filled the page, the indentation inconsistent, as if it had been hastily assembled. Lila angled her body to keep Sarah from seeing. "Sarah, General Marshall wanted to check one last thing with you, too."

As Sarah darted out, her moan straddled the line between annoyed and concerned.

I scanned the list, which began, <I certify that I have agreed to host of my own free will.>

Had someone overheard Sarah saying that Matt would be safe if I did this, her attempted coercion? Or maybe there was a history here no one had mentioned. But now they asked, and I had decided for myself in the end, anyway. I checked it.

<I am aware that I may back out any time up until surgery begins.> Check.

<I am aware that removal of the symbiont following its insertion may result in my death.>

No, Sarah had said no such thing explicitly. She'd only called it permanent, and I'd never asked why. Probable death was enough reason. I looked to see what Lila thought of me reading this, but she watched the door. I paused with my pen over the checkbox, and she caught me.

"It's okay to learn it now. I wanted to make sure you knew."

I nodded acknowledgment and checked.

<Wink if you want out.>

Really? I exed the box without winking. At the bottom, I signed and switched to my notepad. <Is there a reason you're so against this?>

Lila held the clipboard to her chest. "People accuse the Gertewet of manipulation, so we added some oversight. Maybe this will convince them you haven't been brainwashed into accepting it."

I kept my mouth closed and my hands still about what I felt about the information they'd initially withheld and dramatically disclosed. I'd still made the decision for myself.

Another knock brought a woman with long, black hair tied in a bun and medium-dark skin who wore a contrasting white lab coat, someone I'd never met before. "Hi, Ilene? I'm Dr. Bonin, Sarah's doctor."

"One of the base doctors," Lila put in, "but she's got the most experience with symbionts."

"If it's alright with you, I'd like to watch the procedure." Dr. Bonin folded her hands in front of her and looked hopeful.

I almost agreed immediately, but I caught shadows of more people behind her in the bright hall. <How many people are with you?>

Lila glanced out. Her expression set in aggravation, and she slammed the clipboard down. "No." She skirted around Dr. Bonin and out the door. "This is not a traveling circus. Go. You too, Colonel."

"I just want to wish her luck," Jo's voice answered.

"Give her space. You can talk to her tomorrow."

"Good luck!" Jo shouted.

"Go!" Lila returned a minute later. "I'll follow my own advice, too. I just wanted to say, if you need anything, we're here for you."

Lila couldn't know how much Katorin had apparently banked on that in her promises to me about Sarah covering the house. I nodded.

"And don't tell Vinnet that Katorin's our favorite. Not really, but we do like her a lot." She snatched up the clipboard and let herself out, perhaps to guard the door against other invaders.

Sarah passed Lila in the doorway then acknowledged Dr. Bonin. "NFI-Com found out about Mrs. King already."

I straightened.

Sarah shook her head and washed her hands. "Maybe you'll miss them before they get here. They can't reach the rest of the Gertewet, so they're really only my problem."

Katorin hadn't told her about our plan, then.

Sarah seemed to catch my confused expression. "They've got some pretentious name. National Freedom of Information for the Preservation of..."

Dr. Bonin nodded, taking up the rest of the name, "For the Preservation of Constitutional Rights and of Citizen and National Security Commission."

That explained nothing. Whoever NFI-Com was, they might become a thorn in my side. I kept my hands folded over the notebook.

"Are you ready?" Sarah dried her hands, slipped on her gloves, and straightened the sterile placemat she'd laid out earlier, where she staged a small bottle, a scalpel, and something like an oxygen mask.

I bit my lips and nodded. As ready as I could be.

"I, uh..." Sarah bit her lip and fidgeted with her hands. "I really, really, really appreciate you hosting Katorin. I hope we'll become friends, too."

I nodded. Neither Sarah nor Vinnet seemed like people I'd normally choose to spend time with, but they were clearly important to Katorin. Katorin probably had a lot of friends I'd encounter soon, people she'd be leaving behind so that I could support Matt. She didn't seem like she resented that yet, but I hadn't thought about all the implications of her having her own life.

I smiled at Sarah. I didn't have friends in their mid-twenties, but if Katorin was so old, she probably thought of us as the same age.

Dr. Bonin handed me a coarse hospital gown to replace my shirt.

After I changed, Sarah stood by my side and rested a firm hand on my arm with the stiff mannerisms of her alien. "Thank you. The life of a Gertewet is not easy, but we hope you find it fulfilling. As you join us, know that you have not only my and Katorin's personal gratitude but the gratitude of every Gertewet out in the galaxy."

I tensed. It was nice of her to say so, but it made this moment feel so final. Like a benediction. A sacrifice. I put a hand over hers and held tight.

She smiled gently. "You will be well. You'll feel only a minor ache when you wake up with Katorin. She'll take care of you from there."

I nodded. My heart pounded in my ears.

Vinnet instructed me to lie on my stomach, facing the wall. She handed me the face mask, and when I breathed its lavender-and-something-scented gas, consciousness faded.

I barely had time to wonder how big a mistake I'd made.

Chapter Seven

KATORIN

Changing hosts was always hard. Almost every time you lost a partner, a mindmate, and amid that soul-rending grief, you moved in with someone who was afraid of you, who might not believe you are who you say.

I had twelve hours between hosts.

Vinnet visited me for the first half, tea in hand as if she were trying to fill Hartwin's role. Even though she sat in the brilliant white kaxan instead of Hartwin's serene quarters. Even though she couldn't account for my state when the Council doled out my next assignment. We talked about the good times with Setira, the pranks she pulled, the little annoyances that grew endearing in hindsight. We made some order out of the mess of the emotions mixing in the wake of a loss that big. She was almost as good as Hartwin, but no one could process it all in a handful of hours.

I tried to speed through grieving. I figured I had a few days, so when Sarah came to get me two mornings later, I wasn't ready. I hadn't started getting ready.

I went anyway. One doesn't put off a willing host. Ever.

Vinnet had told me that integrating with an Earth brain was a little different. Fortunately, the base brain layout was analogous, plus or minus normal irregularities. The flavor was different. (Not literal flavor—I of course had no tongue. But my hosts did, and I enjoyed flavor. I supposed assessing the slight chemical and structural differences as a flavor was a form of synesthesia.)

Like any mouth taste, I'd get used to it in time.

Biologically, settling into a host came with a burst of adrenaline (to help overcome our otherwise sedentary lifestyle) and dopamine (to reward and reinforce host-taking instincts). I figured this was the only reason I hadn't totally sabotaged a new relationship in my grief.

When Vinnet set me in the warm, welcoming incision, instinct took over, and for a while, everything was simple: the busy, systematic process of placing every neuron tendril about where it ought to go and then, when everything settled, adjusting what didn't feel right.

Ilene remained unconscious. Most hosts dreamed during integration. Sometimes, their subconscious adopted some sort of motif to understand it all, sometimes not. I wasn't settled enough to make sense of what she perceived, let alone how she interpreted it. I hoped it wasn't unpleasant. It added yet another trauma to manage in the tenuous first minutes together.

Finally, I finished and, physically exhausted, listened for the first hints of where her mind and emotions might truly be in unconsciousness.

Her son featured prominently. Her mind drifted on a theme of reclaiming her life: her speech, her financial security, her daily companionship, her ability to provide for her son.

And I could help with that.

But she didn't seem to have understood the cost. She hadn't come to terms with the idea of moving away from Earth. I'd downplayed the dangers inherent in going undercover among Kemtewet too much. She didn't seem to have considered the isolation of being cut off from not only your loved ones but your allies. If we hadn't rushed this...

It was done. We were together now. Hartwin would grant me the new-host grace period to acclimate Ilene. I'd have time to broach the hard topics slowly.

Until then, I could wash dishes and work on her needs. It might even distract me from my latest loss.

Chapter Eight

ILENE

I woke with a headache. It'd been years since my last hangover, and all I wanted to do was lie still and outlast my hammering skull. Unfortunately, something surely needed to be done: hemming or cooking or errands. I blinked my eyes open and stared at the plain, scuffed drywall with a desk lamp on the far side of the room casting my shadow before me. The base. Katorin.

I'd done it.

Bile surged in my throat, sour and stale, and I fought it back down. Irreversible. Invasive. It could expose Matt to new threats. But none of the reasons I'd done it had fallen through. I'd be able to speak. Katorin promised I'd be able to keep Matt safe.

Doubt niggled at the back of my mind like a casserole with too little seasoning. *If he'll be happy there. No, safe is always better than happy.*

What if he wasn't happy in her safehouse? I needed to ask Katorin about that. What if the attack on Earth wasn't as certain as the Gertewet thought—or if the timing wasn't what they thought?

I'm right here. The thought came with a flavor like warm lemon-lime Gatorade and ginger snaps, one repulsive taste and one homey and welcoming.

Was she thinking at me in *flavors?*

Our hosts often associate our connection with a sense. I'm not doing it on purpose. This, with a flavor of fresh bread, basic but wholesome.

Overall, a rather innocuous side effect. At least it signaled which thoughts were Katorin's. I sat up on the medical bed and caught the purple blanket sliding down off my shoulders. Setira's blanket.

Mine. My favorite.

Someone had kept me warm with Katorin's favorite blanket. Even if Sarah only looked out for her symbiont friend, that care encompassed me now, too. I tugged the blanket tight around my drafty shoulders and clung to it. It smelled like the body that was no longer here. *What is your safehouse like?*

It's a whole planet filled with people we smuggled out of the Kemtewet Empire and their descendants. Okay, it's a city. They're not up to galactic technologies, but they're building at their own pace. I'm very proud of them. Her whipped cream flavor soured. *There are few amenities, and it's a lot of indoor living. It's a hard transition for many. My family would take him in, and he'd be well connected.*

Is he in danger or not?

It turned out Katorin didn't have to answer in words. Her mind-sense dithered between fearful tongue-searing spice and nostalgic chocolate cake, and she shared snapshots of memory: visiting Sarah and Maggie, safe at the Rockefellers' house; visiting Sarah and Vinnet at their new house, safe and anonymous from the neighbors. Standing in Black Book's hangar with then-Speaker Rockefeller, past and present Air Force officers, and a sheaf of records she was absolutely certain meant that Earth was in danger.

The flavors settled on a low heat with a base cardboard flavor. *I don't know. The Kem are definitely aiming for Earth, but their timing is unknown. A decade ago, we discovered that they changed their activities to start targeting Earth, but they could take decades more to finish establishing their plans and launch.*

I want to talk to Matt about what he wants.

You can't tell him about the planet until after we're on the way. It will burn bridges if we compromise Percallan security. The Air Force won't allow anyone with awareness of Black Book back onto Earth without operating under their security architecture. Anyone who knew about the Air Force's work with aliens and alien equipment.

I dropped my head into my hands. And of course they wouldn't clear Matt to find out about his potential alternate living arrangements. They'd barely cleared me. I still couldn't articulate why.

Because we're allies, Katorin thought.

They're paying the Gertewet in bodies?

Indignant burnt egg. *They allow recruitment of forces to fight with their allies.*

Katorin had all but said she didn't actually fight. This deal was starting to smell rotten already.

I pushed to my feet, folded the blanket, and laid it on the near-pristine bed. My shirt hung on a hook on the wall, and I pulled it on, cringing as it brushed against my neck. I probed gently, ignoring the pain it sparked. I'd had worse. The whole area was swollen, with particular firmness to the left of my spine that flinched when I touched it. Scabs, natural or chemical, ran along the top in a surgically straight line to a shaved patch at the bottom of my skull.

What was done was done. I shuddered. *I want to see my son.*

Of course. The base's layout unfolded from Katorin's mind, locating not only paths to Sarah's and Jo's offices but also an entire floor full of spaceships, the General's office, and guest quarters and commissary in other buildings.

I checked my appearance once more, grabbed my purse, and reached for the door.

A hint of insecure vanilla wafted from Katorin's mood-flavors, followed by bitter grief. *Would you mind bringing my blanket?*

Of course. I draped it over my arm. I'd left it, because it wasn't mine. It hadn't even occurred me that the owner was now in my body. Odd. The blanket still felt like a stranger's, like I might be caught stealing it.

The hall was empty when I stepped out, the mob of curious well-wishers long vanished. Still, voices murmured from an open office door: Sarah and Lila. Both stood as I entered. Sarah wiped tears away. "Katorin?"

I opened my mouth and thought about trying to answer aloud.

I'll need time, my new symbiont warned. *But I can show you how to sign to her.*

I doubt Sarah knows American Sign Language.

But Vinnet knows both Keidem Sign and the Ger variant.

I thought of what I wanted to say, and after I set the blanket aside, Katorin coached me through the motions. "She's here. We're well."

It wasn't much faster than writing, but it still felt like a win.

Sarah lasted a full second before glomming onto me with a hug. When I didn't respond, she backed off. Her signing, replying to me the way I'd addressed her, was as jerky and uncertain as mine, which leveled the communication playing field for once. She must have been getting coached by her symbiont, too. "Sorry. I'm glad you're both well. Are you going to report in to Hartwing?" Frowning, she tried the sign again. "Hartwin?"

I stiffened and relayed Katorin's response. What a new feeling to be interpreting for someone else instead of them interpreting for me! Or collaborating, at least. "Soon. We need to see to Matt first."

"Right," she breathed out and belatedly signed.

Lila squeezed Sarah's shoulder. "What happened? Didn't it work?"

Sarah pressed her lips together.

I signed an answer from Katorin, and she interpreted it aloud: "Katorin speaks until Ilene can."

Lila closed in. "And? How are you doing, Ilene?"

"Fine," I signed and Sarah interpreted. Fine except for still having an intermediary. I pulled out the notepad.

A loudspeaker in the hall blared, "—tion in the area: incoming kaxan. Unknown Gert—"

This can't be good. Katorin's flavor sense was something like plain oatmeal but grittier.

Sarah and Lila traded wary glances and motioned me to follow them to what Katorin recognized as the hangar. I stopped as soon as I entered and let them forge ahead without me.

Ranks of flying saucers packed the oil-dripped cement, dazzling the eye. Their bulging, mirrored surfaces looked like giant, flattened steel mixing bowls laid out in pairs, as if one were upside down on the other, both stretched out of round. They stood on spindly pegs slightly taller than me with a white circle hanging down from the middle. They would look at home on an X-Files poster or in a grainy photograph, like all that drabble had its kernel of truth here.

My stomach sank.

Of course this kind of world-class secret was classified.

What was I doing in the middle of all this? I'd bitten off more than I could chew.

I caught the sense of soothing, honeyed chamomile from Katorin. *We'll make it work.*

Taking deep breaths, I joined the others in the cool draft at the far end, where they stood behind a row of uniformed men ready to draw their guns. Jo ran up behind me and waited with toe tapping. Always in motion, that Jo.

Now we learn who they send when Vinnet and I are both here, Katorin mused. *If Colonel Patrick doesn't recognize them, then Donn and Teresh must be deployed elsewhere.*

A man appeared in the empty space beside the ship in a burst of dark fog and raised his hands in surrender. He had a tall head like Setira, gray hair gathered straight back, though his anchor beard had turned full white. He was long and wiry, complete with nimble fingers, and wore tight, black pants with an angular leather frock coat.

"Vandrof!" Sarah blurted, turning pink.

Oh, that *Vandrof,* Katorin mused with ginger snaps. Faint memories of Sarah's private confessions leaked from her mind to mine. It seemed he and Vinnet had once been very close. *I never thought I'd meet him.*

I thought there weren't many Gertewet left. Sarah had explained that was why it mattered so much that each symbiont had a host. It sounded like a small community. *I assumed you knew everyone.*

Not from Woods Base.

The dapper old man scanned the crowd, looking puzzled, especially when his gaze returned to Sarah, who stood still, staring.

Vinnet is taking control, Katorin explained. *It looks like Sarah never met him, either.*

Awkward.

A homey kind of awkward.

Even as she thought it, he relaxed, folded his hands behind his back, and waited. He smiled pleasantly at everyone else.

Jo shouldered through. "I assume you're a Gertewet, since our liaison recognized you."

He bowed his head. "Are you the commander here?"

"Second in command."

"My messages are for my colleagues only."

I thought I saw steam pouring out of Jo's ears, but before she could answer, Sarah broke the line of airmen, clasped the newcomer's hands, and planted a kiss on each cheek. "Vandrof, it's Vinnet. We're among friends."

He gripped her hands back and searched her face as if drinking in her appearance. It seemed far too intimate a moment for someone I barely knew and a crowd of security forces.

Isn't he a bit old for her? I wondered.

I'm almost certain he and Vinnet were an item before Sarah was born. Not all old heartthrobs vanish when their hosts age or die.

Maybe my question to Matt yesterday morning needed to be far more literal than I'd meant it. Whatever he thought, I certainly wasn't ready for that.

Good thing my beaus aren't here.

"You'll have to tell me the story of how this happened." Vandrof motioned down her body and then around the room, as if taking in the base in general. "I never expected to be sent to Earth."

"It's a long story." Vinnet stood back and waved me forward. "Katorin is here. What are your messages?"

"Chryson is in urgent need of a host. He expects Sedesh to pass in the next week."

The sudden blast of sour milk sent me digging in my purse for a mint. *What?*

Speaking of old heartthrobs.

Vandrof continued, "Katorin is summoned to the full Council session planned in a week."

The blood froze in my veins. Katorin said we could stay here on Earth with Matt.

We will, she promised. *We'll need to talk to Hartwin first.*

Katorin vaguely promised that she would arrive in time, which obviously confused Vinnet's former lover when I relayed it in sign. Vinnet signed back to wish me a good evening, so I fled to my car. Nothing new, weird, or disturbing happened until I opened the driver's door.

May I drive? Katorin asked.

Do you know how?

You do. It's nearly automatic for you, isn't it?

I scanned the remarkable view of the road from the hangar down to the distant gate. Nearby buildings nestled among the sharp valleys and screening trees on the steep hillside, but much of the base had grown on the prairie below, where straight roads cut across the spring-green flats and ran for miles to the horizon. At this evening hour, hardly any cars dotted the road. *Fine. At least until we reach a main road.*

I shifted to get in the passenger's seat, since I wasn't driving, but paused. Katorin was in my body. *How does this work?*

Sit first.

I climbed into the driver's seat, tossed the blanket to the passenger's side, buckled in, and froze. *Now what?*

I'll take it from here.

Half a minute later, my hand turned the key in the ignition. It felt normal, as if I'd done it, but I was still waiting for Katorin. With my voice, she said, "Start the car."

I didn't trust it. I'd thought I said things right before, when others told me I hadn't.

You will again, Katorin thought and repeated aloud: "You will again."

Put it in drive. Katorin moved the cool, plastic gearshift. "Put it in drive."

I started to believe her. The words sounded the same, and recovery suddenly felt possible in a way that it never had with the flashcards and therapy. Maybe it was only another form of therapy, but a live-in therapist had a lot more on-duty time.

No, she wasn't a cure.

But she'd be a hell of a crutch.

And, when it really counted, when time mattered and I couldn't write a message (or sign to the Gertewet), she could speak for me with an ease Matt never could.

How long are you going to keep repeating what you say?

Until you can do it yourself. "Until you can do it yourself."

I didn't tell her how good that sounded. I didn't have to.

When we're alone, anyway. "When we're alone, anyway."

She narrated each action as she removed the parking brake and pulled out. I tried to mash the brakes a couple times as she made mistakes, but she followed my intentions and acted them out for me, as if I were a lagging backup driver.

I thought you said you could drive. This could end in a wreck.

I'm thinking about it too hard to leave it to the automatic behavior circuits of your brain. She hummed aloud. *I think I'll have to talk about different things.*

And she did, filling the silence with therapy—and handling the car smoothly and safely—for the two-hour drive home. She talked a bit about her dying heartthrob and his symbiont as we raced the train beside the highway, about pranks they'd pulled around their home base with Setira (that Katorin disavowed herself of) while we passed the ruddy buttes. She talked about the family she'd relocated to the safe haven planet Percalli and how proud she was of all they'd built there. It certainly sounded like a pretty safe place.

When we turned off the highway, though, I stopped her. *What am I going to tell Matt?*

She swallowed. *Well, there are options...* "Well, there are options. If we're staying, it would behoove us to nurture our relationship with Black Book. If you told Matt this would cure aphasia, we could make it appear so. Or we can offer to take him to Percalli and tell him everything once he's there."

You said that's a one-way trip. His friends and everything he knows are here. I know you're proud of it, but I don't think he'll be happy there.

Until we perceive... "Until we perceive the danger as imminent, it's better for him to stay here. Very few people are happy about arriving at Percalli."

And I'd been afraid of how Katorin would interfere in my relationship with Matt. Or hurt him. Somehow, having traded only a couple thoughts, we were already on the same page. It hadn't even been this easy with my husband.

My face tightened as Katorin smiled. *Ah, I but I have the advantage...* "I have the advantage. Your husband couldn't read your mind and feel your emotions."

Maybe this could work out.

Chapter Nine

MATT

I'm sure Mom was trying to be nice, asking Aunt Emily to come up from Denver to stay with me while she went for the surgery. But all it meant was that I got stuck at home and constantly thought about what they were doing to Mom while trying not to do anything that annoyed Aunt Emily.

Like pacing the entire house from the kitchen, through the front room Mom used for the business, to the upstairs den. Aunt Emily screeched at me to take it outside. I went back out for a second round after dinner, which is why I saw Mom's headlights turn onto the street.

I bounced on my toes as I watched her pull in.

"Matt!" she yelled as she got out. No biggie; it was the only thing she could say after her stroke. We hugged, and she squeezed tight. "Matt, I love you."

I laughed and pushed back. "What?"

"Matt, I love you. I'm so proud of you."

She said full sentences!

It had been impossible, but she'd done it. They'd broken this last year of her silence.

The sun had set, so at least the neighbors couldn't see the tears on my face. I wiped them off on my shoulder anyway. I had to try twice to push anything out past the frog in my throat. "It worked! Mom, it actually worked! That was so fast."

The doctors all said it would be months or years before she re-learned how to talk. As of this morning, she'd gotten maybe twenty words back. And now... I hugged her again. "Is it just a few words?"

"No, it's everything. You're going to get tired of hearing me—"

"How is that possible? How did you get an accent?"

I let her go and caught her sucking her lips sheepishly in a way I hadn't seen before—or at least not that I remembered since Dad died. She shook her head dismissively. "That's just the way it is. Let's go in. What are you even doing out here in the dark, Kid Commando?"

I put up with her mussing my hair and followed her into the house. As she passed the front porch light, I thought I saw something differ-ent about the back of her neck. Certainly, they hadn't shaved around the crown of her head for whatever surgery, which was weird. Even weirder that she wasn't telling me everything she knew, though she had been a little cagey about it since she first met with the Air Force.

My throat tightened.

She made this devil's deal. What did she have to pay for it?

Aunt Emily rushed out of the kitchen, hands wringing, while I closed the door. "Did it work?"

Mom spread her hands. "Perfectly."

Aunt Emily covered her mouth with her hands. "Thank God! But you have an accent!"

Mom shrugged. "A slight side effect. Maybe it will go away in time."

"This is such a miracle! And they gave you a job, too?"

"Let's talk about that upstairs in a minute. We need drinks." Mom disappeared into the kitchen, probably rummaging for her iced tea.

A couch summoning. Immediately after she got home. I swallowed past the hard lump in my throat. Aunt Emily and I both hovered in the kitchen doorway, watching Mom fill the kettle. Hot chocolate discussions were even worse than cold drinks discussions.

"What was the surgery like?" Aunt Em prodded. "It must have gone well. I'm surprised you drove yourself home."

Mom rubbed her neck absently and rolled her shoulders as if they were stiff. "They were actually well practiced at this surgery, so they had a good handle on the recovery time."

"You said you'd be home an hour ago." I tugged my hoodie strings tight.

"Some things came up afterwards." Mom dug out the Godiva hot chocolate from the back of the drawer, completely bypassing our regular stuff. "Matt, turn around."

I did, crossing my arms. It wasn't like I didn't know she kept the booze over the fridge. But hot chocolate *and* mix-ins? I stiffened. Whatever was going on was bad.

In a couple minutes, she armed us with drinks and marched us upstairs. Aunt Emily took one of the spindly antique armchairs by the window. I left my mug on the coffee table, so it didn't spill as I lowered myself onto the couch—no use pissing Mom off on top of whatever else was going on.

She sat on the edge of the cushion and wavered between setting her mug down or warming her hands on it.

I twirled the loose thread on the couch arm. "So, what's so bad about your new job?"

"I didn't say anything was bad."

Her accent was so weird, I couldn't begin to place it.

"You got the impossible, instant cure, and you came home and suddenly made hot chocolate," I pointed out.

"I need to go on a work trip next week."

"Okay?" People's parents went on work trips all the time, didn't they? Though everyone else had two parents—okay, not *everyone*. "I didn't know you were going to travel in this job."

She sucked her lips in that weird expression and stared at the carpet. "It should only be a day or two this time."

It'd been weird having her gone today, but I could do a day or two, right? Jonny Malone got his house to himself sometimes when his parents went to visit his sister in college. "Where are you going?"

"I can't say."

"Is it going to be dangerous?"

"No." She still didn't look up. "We'll be perfectly safe. It will be a brief trip."

"That's what you said." I stared at her. Maybe she felt like she had to repeat herself, now that everything she said wasn't written down.

"Em, can you stay with Matt?"

Not even asking me what I wanted. This wasn't like her.

Aunt Em shook her head. "It sounds like the timing is uncertain. What if he came down to stay with us?"

Mom nodded.

I snatched my mug up and almost burned my tongue. I set it back down, sloshing on the table. "Is it going to be like this from now on?"

She laid a hand on my shoulder and looked me in the eye. It'd been over a year since she could do that while answering. "No. It should only be once. I need to make a request."

"Can't you call?"

"It must be in person."

Weird. Who said "must"?

She rubbed my shoulder. "It's just a couple days, and then it will all be settled."

"What's with the hot chocolate, then?"

Chapter Ten

KATORIN

"What's with the hot chocolate, then?" Matt asked me. Us.

It wasn't for Matt. Or Em. It never had been. Ilene was panicking, not wanting to leave Matt to travel all across the galaxy for a couple days. But we could get off the duty roster and come back and be sure that if he stayed here in the path of Kem expansion, we could at least stand by to evacuate him if the time came.

Ilene didn't want to leave—not today, not next week. And apparently not ever.

This was supposed to stabilize our lives.

But Gertewet life simply wasn't stable the way she wanted.

Across the room in one of the fancy sitting chairs by the floral curtain-framed window, Ilene's sister Em licked her lips. "I think my drink is a little hot. I'm going to put some ice in it."

Odd timing.

She's excusing herself to give me space with Matt, Ilene interpreted.

Em collected her flowing skirt and her mug and left. The stairs creaked to mark her passage.

Matt still glared at us over his drink.

I don't know what to do, kid, Ilene thought. *This all seemed so clear this morning.*

It will be fine. My host and I always got through this stage. With effort. I sighed deeply, willing the anxiety and frustration out with breath. "Let me be honest with you, Matt."

You, too, Ilene.

"It's been an extremely stressful couple of days. I think this will be better for all of us in the long run. I knew I was going to have to ask for unusual accommodations. I'll go, sort it out, and come right back."

"And then what's going to change?"

I froze. Everything. Nothing. All the little orbits of life shifted with a new gravitational mass in the relationship balance.

Before I could answer, Ilene demanded, *What if Sarah won't pay the mortgage?*

Vinnet will.

What if Matt needs me?

You're right here.

That wasn't enough reassurance for her. *Are you going to handle all my calls instead of Matt?*

It would be efficient.

What are we going to do all day with this fake new job with the Air Force?

If you don't want to continue sewing full time, Black Book is always happy to have a second Gertewet to collaborate with. I sipped Ilene's "Bailey'ed" hot chocolate, hoping it would soothe her nerves. It didn't seem to help, and I wondered why she'd insisted on it. *We will work this one challenge at a time and adjust with feedback. No one is risking death. This will be a relaxed phase to acclimate to one another.*

I wrapped her hands around the warm mug. They didn't ache like Setira's had. They felt like they had much finer control, good for constructing bombs, not that I was likely to build any soon. I tried smiling at Matt. "What's going to change is that you and I can talk, and we'll leave aphasia as a mere memory. I might need to make an occasional trip, but they'll be short."

"Do you need to, like, go to work now?"

Ah, the consequences of Sarah's clumsy fumbling around the Air Force's secrecy. "I'll negotiate my hours. I'll be here for you, kiddo."

I squeezed the mug tighter. *We should see if we can park a kaxan at the house. The drive to the base is too long for an emergency.*

It won't fit in the garage, Ilene worried. *The neighbors will see it.*

It cloaks. I set the mug on one of Ilene's spare-fabric coasters. I always forgot new humans weren't used to constant change. I shifted down the comfortably worn-in couch and wrapped an arm around Matt's tense shoulders. "Hey, kid, got a question for you."

He stared into his full drink. "What?"

"Can I still write to you sometimes?"

"Huh?" He looked up.

"If you don't want things to change, how about we don't change it all at once?"

He shrugged.

Your turn, I thought and yielded control to my host. She clearly needed it, and so did he.

Her hands shook as she reached for the whiteboard behind our mug. Her body relaxed as she moved, the way new hosts' often did as they realized we weren't going to act like Kem and control them all the time. As they got used to switching. She leaned her shoulder against Matt's as she wrote.

<Some things are going to change. But I still love you. I'm still coming back to be here for you. And like K—> She erased her slip, and I hated that she had to. I liked my new families to get to know me. <Like I said, we don't have to change all at once.>

He leaned into her now, relaxing in a way he hadn't with me, as if he could tell us apart already. It probably hadn't risen to conscious awareness yet.

Ilene basked in that contact. *Finally. I can support him instead of him supporting me.*

"Promise?" he asked.

<I promise.>

Epilogue

MATT

The house was quiet with Mom in her bedroom and Aunt Emily settled into the pull-out bed in the den. Only the occasional bump sounded over the low gush of the vents.

I flopped on my bed—no gentlemanly sitting this late at night—and stared at the popcorn-textured ceiling.

Mom came home safe.

That was the important thing. The impossible thing that contradicted everything the doctors had ever told us and all common sense. Somehow, she could speak. She wasn't going to need me anymore. Already, it felt like she was leaving me behind. She hadn't asked me to call Aunt Emily about coming up during the surgery. She hadn't wanted me to help her call Sarah but had actually tried emailing her.

All of a sudden, she didn't need me anymore.

I rolled over and smashed my face into the pillow. Mom had made the soft pillowcase to match the wizard blanket she'd expanded into a quilt. I clutched the edge of the quilt.

Why'd she have to do it? She was fine. Why did Dad have to die? Why couldn't the drunk driver have stayed at home or passed out at the bar? Why couldn't Dad have driven slower or faster or not been at the wrong intersection at the wrong time?

I wiped my tears on the pillow.

Better not to think about that.

Mom was staying, she said.

But if she commuted to the Air Force all the time, she wouldn't really be here. She wouldn't be tailoring anymore. She wouldn't be working downstairs when I got home and there to listen to the carp from school. She wouldn't need me to call customers back or make appointments or anything, really.

She wouldn't need me.

Except.

Her whole deal still felt fishy.

And her sudden accent didn't make any sense. How did they fix aphasia and give her an accent she'd never had before, one I'd never even heard?

That wasn't right.

I wiped my eyes again, pulled out my notebook, and updated my evidence list.

Acknowledgements

Immense thanks as always to Shell for fantastic feedback, motivating discussions, and tireless cheerleading. Immense gratitude also to Iris Matthews, Corinna Lawson, Tara L. Roi, and Bethany J. Miller, who not only gave hard feedback but also helped find a way for Ilene to be a more realistic mother. (If, perhaps, still a little frustrating.) Also to Athena Falcon for detailed feedback to polish this little novella. And to Dex Greenbright for supernatural patience.

Thanks to Ryan Hodros and KM Herkes for their support.

Thanks to Seton Hill University's Writing Popular Fiction program, I was able to transform a 2019 draft to something better, connect to a broader pool of critiquers—with just the right experience to pinpoint the major problem—and implement smoother prose than I'd previously aspired to. Similarly, thanks to Case Western Reserve University for offering a freshman neurolinguistics class and to Athena for vetting my application of it.

One last thanks to Ms. Ilene for wisdom and for making a safe space for teens to ask hard questions. Ilene King isn't you, but I hope she honors your memory. Also in loving memory of Grandmother Balinskas; I only met you briefly, but I saw your struggles and now follow in your footsteps of making life work in spite of new bodily limitations.

Finally, everlasting gratitude to my mom for setting such a relent-lessly brave example in uncertain times. You always deserved to be happy.

Afterword

Thank you, dear reader, for embarking on a very different adventure from *Rights of Use*. Your regularly scheduled action/adventure scifi will be back with *Laws Among Friends*, but Matt and Ilene have been on my heart since high school. I wanted to stretch my legs on more character-focused stories.

Bear with me in this series. I plan to keep experimenting with storytelling and giving you more surprises.

Glossary

aphasia – the state of the brain losing some or much capacity for language

ASL – American Sign Language

Gertewet (Ger) – body-sharing symbionts fighting the oppressive Kemtewet ("G is for good")

kaxan – small, interstellar transport, often colloquially referred to as a "flying saucer"

Kemtewet (Kem) – evil body-possessing parasites ("K is for kill")

lifeport – an emergency tank for symbionts that provides some virtual link to the outside world

NFI-Com – National Freedom of Information for the Preservation of Constitutional Rights and of Citizen and National Security Commission

Dramatis Personae

Family

Matt King – teenage advocate

Ilene King – Matt's mother

Emily "Em" – Ilene's sister

Project Black Book, US Air Force

General Renee Marshall – Project Black Book commanding officer

Colonel Jo Patrick – Air Force officer at Project Black Book

Sarah Anderson – Gertewet liaison

Dr. Bonin – Air Force physician for alien symbionts and hosts

Lila Wijesekara – Air Force host recruit ombudsperson

Gertewet

Katorin – Gertewet operative, courier

Setira – Katorin's human host

Vinnet – Gertewet operative, host recruiter

Sarah Anderson – Vinnet's human host

Vandrof – Gertewet operative

Chryson – Gertewet operative

Sedesh – Chryson's human host

Teresh – Gertewet operative

Hartwin – Plains Base Coordinator

Donn Marshall – human host to Kitchell, Gertewet operative

Kemtewet

Cube Head – captured alien